MEGAN'S BIRTHDAY TREE

A STORY ABOUT OPEN ADOPTION

Laurie Lears

Illustrated by Bill Farnsworth

Albert Whitman & Company, Morton Grove, Illinois

To Betty and Vernon Morris.
With special thanks to my editor, Abby Levine—L.L.

For Allison.—B.F.

Library of Congress Cataloging-in-Publication Data

Lears, Laurie.
Megan's birthday tree : a story about open adoption / by Laurie Lears ;
illustrated by Bill Farnsworth.
p. cm.
Summary: Every year on Megan's birthday, her birth mother, Kendra, sends a
picture of the tree she planted the day Megan was born, so when Kendra
decides to get married and move to a new house, Megan worries that she will be forgotten.
ISBN 0-8075-5036-1 (hardcover)
[1. Adoption--Fiction. 2. Mothers and daughters--Fiction.
3. Moving, Household--Fiction. 4. Trees--Fiction.] I. Farnsworth, Bill, ill. II. Title.
PZ7.L46365Me 2005   [Fic]--dc22   2004018583

The design is by Carol Gildar.

For more information about Albert Whitman & Company,
please visit our web site at www.albertwhitman.com.

About Open Adoption

"Sometimes I wonder about my adoption. But I don't have to go far to find answers to my questions." The opening lines to this story reveal both the essence of how open adoptions work and why openness is so beneficial to a child's sense of self. In an open adoption, birth and adoptive families meet, get to know each other, and agree to maintain some form of meaningful contact. While the frequency and form of contact will vary, an open adoption relationship establishes an important connection between birth and adoptive families that serves to surround the child with love and support.

As recently as fifteen years ago, closed adoptions were the norm for all adoptions in the United States. Today, the majority of American infants placed into adoptive homes will have the benefit of ongoing contact with their birth families.

When Kendra, Megan's birth mother, hugs Megan, saying, "You will always be a part of me," she reflects the deep-seated love of birth parents for the children they have placed into adoptive families. In making the hardest decisions of their lives, birth parents have as their goal to provide a better life for their child than they are in a position to offer. A shared love for this child binds together all parties in an adoption. In an open adoption relationship, this love is simply and openly acknowledged.

Jane Page, M.S.W., L.C.S.W.
Clinical Director of Adoption Services
The Cradle, Evanston, Illinois

Sometimes I wonder about my adoption. But I don't have to go far to find answers to my questions. Mom and Dad tell me what I want to know. And since I have an open adoption, I stay in touch with my birth mother, Kendra, too. Although I don't see her often, we mail each other lots of notes and photos. I keep everything Kendra sends me in a big box on my shelf.

I especially like to look at the photos of the Birthday Tree. That's the little tree Kendra planted in her yard after I was born. She says the tree reminds her of me and the way I'm growing. Each year on my birthday, Kendra decorates the tree and mails me a photo of it. And every year that tree grows taller!

One day Kendra sends me a note that says:

Dear Megan,
I have some exciting news! I am getting married in two months! I'll be moving to a different town. I'll come to see you and your family on the way to my new home.
Love, Kendra

My stomach turns upside down. All I can think of is the Birthday Tree. Kendra will have to leave it behind when she moves. What if Kendra forgets me, without the tree to remind her?

I want to ask Mom my question. But
the words get stuck in my throat. Instead I say,
"Tell me the story of when I was born."

Mom pulls me onto her lap like she always does when
she tells the story. "Kendra counted every one of your fingers
and toes," she says. "Then she kissed the top of your head and
began to cry. Kendra loved you so much! Yet she knew she
wasn't ready to take care of a baby, so she'd chosen Dad and
me to be your parents."

I snuggle closer to Mom. "I'm glad you and Dad
adopted me," I say, "but I hope Kendra always remembers me."

"Kendra would never forget you!" says Mom.

I'm still worried, though. I'd feel better if Kendra could
take the Birthday Tree with her when she moves.

On Saturday, Dad trims the bushes and trees in our yard. As I gather up the branches, an idea pops into my head. "Dad, do you think one of these branches could grow into a tree?" I ask.

"Hmmm, I don't know about that," he says.

But I'm already running inside with a branch. I place it in a jar of water like I've seen Mom do with her plant cuttings.

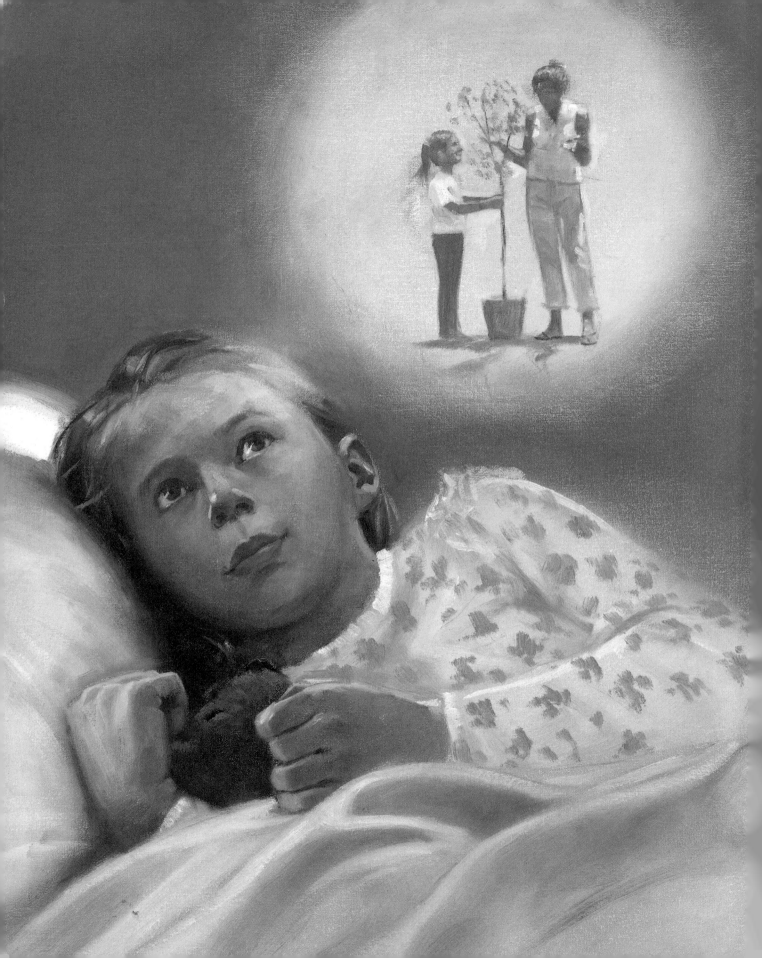

That night I lie awake thinking of how I will put the branch into a pot of soil after it grows roots. By the time Kendra comes to visit, the branch will be a little tree! Kendra can plant the tree in her new yard to remind her of me.

I wait and wait for the branch to grow roots. But nothing happens. Finally the water in the jar turns the color of apple juice and begins to stink. I gently dump the branch outside. I'll have to find another way to get a tree for Kendra.

The next time Mom and I go to the grocery store, I stop to look at the plants and flowers for sale. All at once I have an idea. "Do you sell any trees?" I ask the lady behind the counter.

"No, but Walton's Garden Center does," she says.

That's it! I will save my money and buy a tree for Kendra!

I don't even spend the dollar that I brought along for a treat. I take it home and drop it into my piggy bank.

I earn money by doing extra chores around the house.
I help Dad fold laundry and clear out the garage.

I help Mom wash the car and straighten up the closets.

I even take our next-door neighbor's dog, Pinky, for a walk every day after school.

When Dad decides to go to Walton's Garden Center to buy vegetable seeds, I rush upstairs to get the money from my piggy bank. I'm so excited I can hardly sit still in the car.

At Walton's, I slip away to find the trees. They look so beautiful! I close my eyes and imagine one of them growing straight and tall in Kendra's new front yard.

I choose a tree with long branches that reach toward the sky. But when I look at the price tag, I almost stop breathing! I don't have nearly enough money to pay for this tree . . . or any of the others.

I swallow the lump in my throat and shuffle back to Dad.

"Are you okay, Megan?" he asks.

I hold tight to Dad's warm, strong hand. "I want to buy a new Birthday Tree for Kendra . . . only they cost too much," I say.

Dad offers me some money from his wallet.

"No, thank you," I say. "I want to get the tree by myself."

A few days later, I notice a scraggly tree growing in our yard. "Look," I say to Dad. "This tree isn't getting much sun because of the bigger trees behind it. Do you think I could dig it up for Kendra?"

"It would take a lot of digging, but you could try," says Dad.

I set right to work. After a while my arms are so stiff I have to jiggle them loose.

"Want some help?" asks Dad.

But I shake my head and pick up the shovel again.

The next day, while I'm digging, I hear someone pull into the driveway. When I look up, I see Kendra hurrying across the yard.

"Megan!" she calls. "What are you doing?"

I forget all about being sweaty and dirty as I run to meet her. "I . . . I'm trying to dig up a tree for you," I say. "I didn't want you to forget me after you got married and moved to a new house."

At first Kendra looks confused. But then she wraps her arms around me and holds me close. "Oh, Megan, I don't need a tree or anything else to remember you! Even though we don't live together, you will always be a part of me."

And when I see the tears in Kendra's eyes, I know she really means it.

"I guess I'm kind of silly," I say as we walk back to the house together.

"Well, I guess you got that from me," she says, pointing to the back of her truck.

I can hardly believe my eyes! The whole bed of the pickup is filled with a tree. A big tree . . . the Birthday Tree!

"I want to be able to send you photos on your birthdays," says Kendra.

I have a million questions to ask Kendra. Like how she ever dug up that tree! But for now my questions will have to wait. Mom and Dad are hugging Kendra, and I'm squeezed right in the middle!

I don't mind, though. I'm thinking how lucky I am to be part of such a special family.